THE FOG MOUND

2

FARADAWN

THE FOG MOUND, BOOK #1:
TRAVELS OF THELONIOUS

COMING SOON
THE FOG MOUND, BOOK #3:
SIMON'S DREAM

THE FOG MOUND

2

FARADAWN

SUSAN SCHADE *and* JON BULLER

Aladdin Paperbacks
New York   London   Toronto   Sydney

ALADDIN PAPERBACKS
An imprint of Simon & Schuster Children's Publishing Division
1230 Avenue of the Americas, New York, NY 10020
Copyright © 2007 by Susan Schade and Jon Buller
All rights reserved, including the right of reproduction in whole or in part in any form.
ALADDIN PAPERBACKS and related logo are registered trademarks of Simon & Schuster, Inc.
Also available in a SIMON & SCHUSTER BOOKS FOR YOUNG READERS hardcover edition.
Designed by Daniel Roode
The text of this book was set in Geometric 415.
Manufactured in the United States of America
First Aladdin Paperbacks edition June 2008
4 6 8 10 9 7 5
01 14 QGT
The Library of Congress has cataloged the hardcover edition as follows:
Schade, Susan.
Faradawn / Susan Schade and Jon Buller.
p. cm. (Fog Mound; bk. 2)
Summary: Continues the adventures of Thelonious the chipmunk and his friends,
who meet a human, build a boat, and go searching for the land called Faradawn.
[1. Chipmunks—Fiction. 2. Animals—Fiction. 3. Adventure and adventurers—Fiction.
4. Science fiction.] I. Buller, Jon, 1943—II. Title.
PZ7.S3314Far2007
[Fic]—dc22
2005037867
ISBN-13: 978-0-689-87686-8 (hc.)   ISBN-10: 0-689-87686-6 (hc.)
ISBN-13: 978-0-689-87687-5 (pbk.)   ISBN-10: 0-689-87687-4 (pbk.)

For Wylene, Sara, Doris, and Ruth

Visit Susan Schade and Jon Buller at their website:
www.bullersooz.com

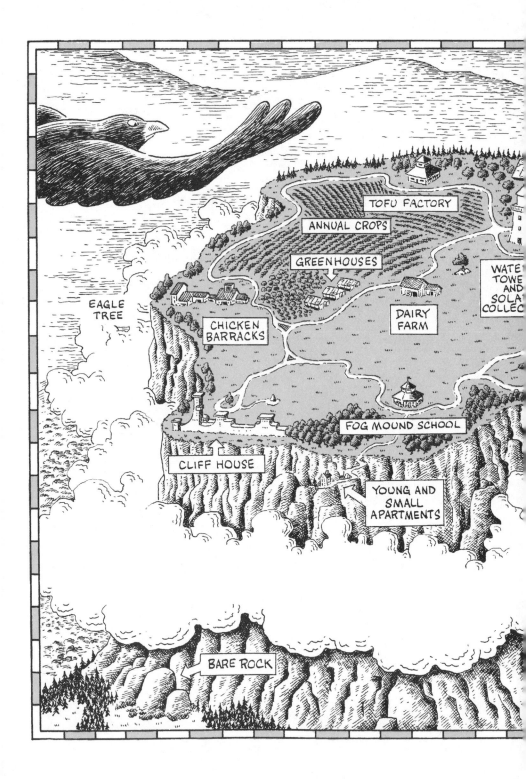

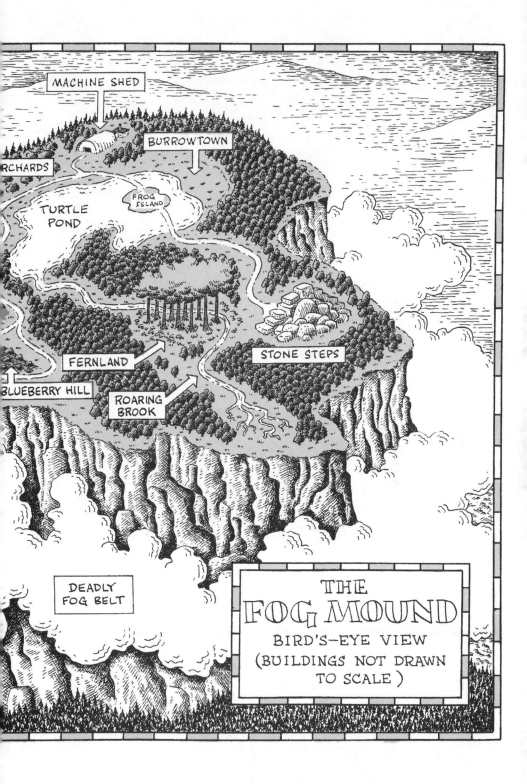

MACHINE SHED

ORCHARDS

BURROWTOWN

FROG ISLAND

TURTLE POND

FERNLAND

BLUEBERRY HILL

ROARING BROOK

STONE STEPS

DEADLY FOG BELT

THE
FOG MOUND
BIRD'S-EYE VIEW
(BUILDINGS NOT DRAWN
TO SCALE)

My adventures began
with an unexpected trip
down the river,
into unknown territory,

where I discovered the legendary
City of Ruins,

and where I met Fitzgerald,
a book-loving porcupine;

Olive, a vegetarian bear
who was "good with engines";

and Brown,
a talking lizard.

Together, we four escaped
by velocicopter

from the evil Dragon Lady
and her army of ratminks.

Unfortunately, we left behind our
map of the Secret Way, and almost
got lost in the deadly fog.

But we were saved by Brown,
and then we found a shrunken man
inside a freezing chamber—the
world's last living human!

After we had thawed him out, Bill showed us the rest of the way, through the labyrinth, to Olive's lovely home on the Fog Mound.

But Bill himself remained a mystery, saying nothing except one word, and that word was . . .

1

The Cliff

LIVING ON THE FOG MOUND IS GREAT! THERE'S NO HUNTING OR KILLING. AND THE MOUND IS PROTECTED BY A BAND OF DEADLY FOG, SO NOBODY CAN GET IN UNLESS THEY KNOW THE SECRET WAY. WHAT COULD BE SAFER?

BROWN!

AND CLUID! WAIT UP! I'LL BE RIGHT OUT!

9

OH NO, BROWN! HE'S FALLEN INTO THE **DEADLY FOG**! IT WILL MAKE HIM CRAZY AND HE'LL NEVER GET OUT!

NO, IT'S OKAY. I CAN SEE HIM.

HE'S LANDED IN A BUSH, JUST ABOVE THE FOG.

I WON'T FALL. AND DON'T FORGET, THE FOG DOESN'T AFFECT ME, BECAUSE I'M A REPTILE.

CLUID, CAN YOU RUN AND GET OLIVE? TELL HER TO BRING A LONG ROPE AND A BASKET.

OKAY.

12

16

2

Suspicion

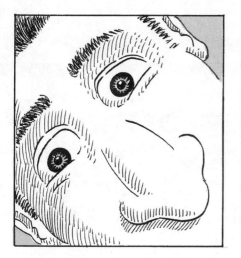

After my rescue by basket, Olive made me lie down on one of the huge beds that the humans had left behind in Cliff House.

I woke up to find a pair of blue eyes staring at me—human eyes.

I said, "Hello, Bill."

As usual, Bill didn't answer. I wasn't surprised. Bill had only spoken once in the whole time I had known him. He *did* look pleased to see that I was awake, though. And for once I had his attention.

I thought I would try asking him some questions.

"So, Bill," I said, "what did you mean when you said, 'Faradawn'?"

He looked at me intently.

"Is it a place?" I asked.

Bill nodded.

I sat up. That was the first time Bill had ever responded to a direct question!

"Is it a place like the Fog Mound?" I asked him. "Where the animals grow their own food?"

He stared off into space.

I didn't want to lose his attention. There was so much I wanted to ask him. I decided to try simpler questions.

"Bill!" I said.

He turned back to me.

19

"Did you used to be big?"

He looked down at his own small hands, pointed at himself and at me, and laughed.

I took that to be a yes. We animals were pretty sure of it, anyway, because of the big clothes we had found in the freezing chamber with him.

"Did you shrink in the freezing chamber?" I asked him.

He laughed again and shrugged.

I took that to mean, *I guess so.*

I said, "Did you used to be . . . uh . . . smarter?"

No answer.

Bill could be very annoying.

I tried a different question. "Were there other humans here in olden times?"

Bill laughed.

I glared at him.

"I wish you would talk," I complained. "I'll bet you used to talk before you got frozen, and there's a lot I want to know! Like, who made the Fog Mound? Was it you? And what was it like back then, when humans ruled the earth? And what happened to them, anyway?"

Bill licked his lips, but he didn't say anything.

I waited a few moments, just in case he was going to speak, but he

started staring off into space again.

"Still not talking, huh?"

Bill and I both turned quickly.

The speaker was Fitzgerald Porcupine. He was standing in the doorway and frowning at Bill.

Olive Bear was there too.

"How are you feeling, Thelonious?" Olive asked, coming in and sitting on the bed.

Brown and Cluid trooped in behind her and climbed up the bed quilt.

"I feel fine," I said. "I was just talking to Bill here . . ."

I gestured toward where Bill had been, but he wasn't there.

"What happened to Bill?" I said.

Everyone looked around. Bill had vanished.

"I wonder where he went," I said. "I thought I was getting somewhere with him."

"Bill likes Thelonious," Brown explained to the others.

"Well, you guys share a room with him," Fitzgerald grumbled. "You must have had plenty of chances to talk to him there."

"We hardly ever see him," I said.

"He *sleeps* there," Brown added. "But that's about it."

"Oh?" Fitzgerald sounded suspicious. "What does he do all day? Where does he go?"

Brown and I looked at each other and shrugged. "I try to keep an eye on him so he doesn't get hurt," I said, "but he keeps wandering off."

"Do *you* know where he goes, Olive?" Fitz asked her.

"No," she replied. "I never see him. I know that my father tried to interview him a few times, and that he couldn't get any information out of him. I think he's decided that Bill is harmless."

"Hah!" Fitzgerald said. "It's true that he doesn't seem very bright. But I don't like these disappearances. He makes me nervous. Humans can't be trusted, you know."

He pulled on his whiskers. "I say he should be watched," he added.

"I thought you liked and respected the humans and all they had accomplished," I said.

"Well, they did do some amazing things, it's true," he admitted.

"They built the City of Ruins," I reminded him, "and everything in it."

"They didn't build the City of Ruins," he corrected me. "They built a beautiful city and then they deserted it, and it *became* the City of Ruins."

"You and Brown must miss living there," Cluid said.

"Not me," Brown grunted.

But Fitzgerald sighed. "I do miss some things about it," he said. "My old bookshop and my old friends, for instance. And the City is always interesting. It's got buildings I've never explored, human artifacts still waiting to be discovered, canned foods I haven't tried yet. And from time to time strange animals turn up—new friends." He looked at me and Olive.

"I'd like to see it," Cluid said. "And I'd like to see Thelonious's old home too—the Untamed Forest."

"There's no place as good as the Fog Mound," I said loyally.

But the truth was, I would have loved to travel again. I began thinking about the old days back home—running naked through the forest with my friend Victor, and telling scary tales at the All-Forest Meets; and in the City of Ruins—riding on Fitzgerald's scooter with the wind in my fur, zipping around a pile of rubble to find a beautiful iron fence or a smooth marble statue.

"Olive would like to travel again, wouldn't you, Olive?" Cluid asked.

"Would you, Olive?" I said. "I thought you were so happy to be home."

"Well . . ." Olive wandered over to the window and looked out.

"The truth is, I've been worried about my sister, Ruby. I've already lost one sister. I would hate to lose Ruby, too. And she's been gone a long time now. I *have* thought some of going off the Mound again, Thelonious—of going to look for Ruby."

"There's that place called Faradawn that Bill mentioned," I said. "We could go there, too!"

"Bill!" Fitzgerald snorted. "I wouldn't pay any attention to anything Bill says. *I* never heard about any place called Faradawn."

"I still don't see what you've got against Bill," I said.

"I like humans fine, where they belong—in the past! I just don't want to share the planet with them! The humans kept animals as pets, you know, and they experimented on them too. You should know that,

Thelonious, from that legend you like so much, the one where Bob Human saves the animals from the mad scientist."

I looked at him. "That's just an old legend," I said. But I wondered. In my earlier travels I had discovered that some of the old legends were true. Could *The Story of Bob* be true too?

Fitzgerald turned from me to Brown, and back to me. "Are you two careful about what you say in front of Bill?"

"I never think about it," I said. "Besides, what could we possibly say that he doesn't know already? We're new here, don't forget. And Bill probably built the whole Fog Mound!"

"We don't know that," Fitzgerald said. "He could have been an *enemy* scientist! Maybe the scientist who built the Fog Mound froze Bill because he was a threat! Did you ever think of that?"

I had to admit that I had never thought of that.

"He should be watched," Fitzgerald repeated. "And Thelonious, you and Brown are just the ones to do it. Find out where he goes when he disappears, and what he does when he gets there!"

3

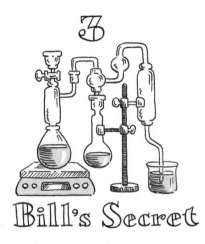

Bill's Secret

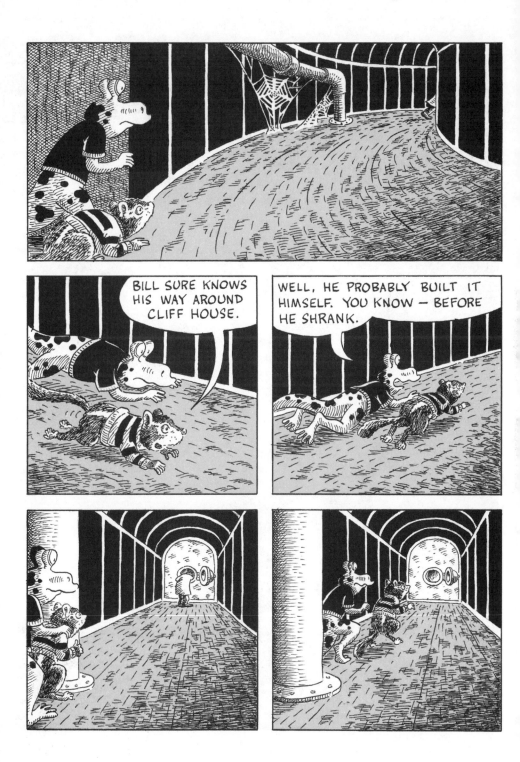

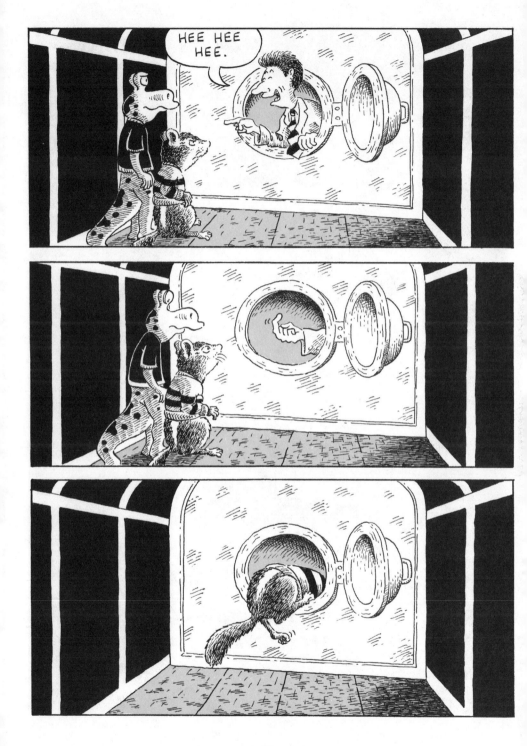

33

4

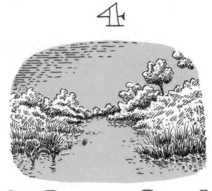

On Roaring Brook

It was a boat! And even Fitzgerald had to admit that it was beautiful. *I* thought it was perfect in every detail, right down to the name painted on the bow—*Heloise*. And that was before we even knew the full extent of her perfection!

"It's lovely!" Olive said, bending over to touch the small boat. "It looks like some kind of waterproofed fabric stretched over a wooden frame. Interesting. I wonder if it will float."

Some small tools lay on the table beside the boat, along with some shavings and piles of sawdust. Olive picked up a drill.

"Microtools!" she said, feeling the tip with her thumb. "I could have used these when I was putting together my model airplane."

She turned to Bill. "Did you build this yourself, Bill?" she asked.

Bill beamed proudly.

I liked the tools. They were small enough for Bill's tiny hands (or for mine) and very sharp and shiny. I wondered where Bill had gotten them, and whether he would let me borrow them sometime.

I sidled up to *Heloise* and ran my paw along the stretched fabric. Imagine Bill coming here and working on her every day! Even with his little tools, it must have been hard for him now that he was so small.

He couldn't even get up to his work surface without a ladder! And he must have made that ladder himself, by screwing boards on to a broom handle. I wondered how he got it up here against the table.

There's more to Bill than meets the eye, I thought.

Brown and I climbed aboard *Heloise*, sat in the cockpit, and made believe we were paddling.

"Is she seaworthy?" I asked Bill.

Bill laughed. Then he pointed at me. "For you," he said.

"For me?"

"Boat for Thelonious," he said carefully. His voice, unused to speech, scratched a little.

I gasped. Did he mean it? *Me?*

Then Bill pointed to Olive and cleared his throat. "Olive build big," he said.

We all looked at Olive.

"You want me to build a big version of this boat?" she asked Bill.

Bill nodded and cleared his throat. "We will travel by boat," he announced. He gave us a big smile, then backed down his broom-handle ladder, walked over to a dusty pillow on the floor, and curled up and went to sleep.

We were all stunned.

Fitzgerald grumbled, "So, now he's telling everyone what to do? Who does he think he is? The boss of us?"

"We will travel by boat." Brown repeated Bill's words. "Where do you think he wants us to go? That place he said before? What was it, Fardawn?"

"Faradawn," I said.

We all looked at the sleeping human.

"At least he's talking more," I said. "Maybe he'll explain after he's rested."

The next day Olive carried my boat to Roaring Brook. The rest of us trotted along beside her big feet. I was so excited!

Fitz carried the picnic basket.

When we got there, we all crowded around the edge of the brook.

Olive set *Heloise* gently on the water.

Would she sink? Or would she float?

She floated!

She bobbed around like a proud brown duck, tugging at her line. Olive pulled her steady against the bank, and held her there so Brown and I could climb in.

"WAIT!" Bill ordered.

We all turned to look at him.

He held up one finger, then climbed into the picnic basket.

"Now what?" said Fitzgerald.

We waited.

Soon Bill reappeared, trying to pull a small sack out of the basket.

"Let me help you with that." Olive lifted the sack and put it on the ground.

Bill climbed down, opened the sack, and pulled out two corks with straps attached to them. Holding one up against his back, he pulled the strap around his tummy to demonstrate. Then he pointed at me and Brown.

"Life preservers!" Olive exclaimed. "So you won't drown if you fall in the water. Good idea, Bill."

"But I don't need any life preserver!" I protested. "I can swim!"

"So can I," said Brown.

"Bill is right," said Olive. "You never know. You could get a cramp or hit your head. Better to be safe than sorry."

Brown rolled his eyes at me, but we strapped on our life preservers.

Olive gave the boat a little push, and *Heloise* floated away from the shore.

Brown and I took up our paddles.

Of course, none of us had ever paddled a boat before. But Fitzgerald, who had read human books about sailors, kept shouting instructions, like "Hard alee!" and "Haul on the bowline!" and "Come about, come about!"

Even with all our splashing and turning in circles, *Heloise* didn't take on a drop of water, and after a while Brown and I managed to get her to the opposite shore.

"Hooray!" yelled Cluid.

"Avast, ye mateys!" yelled Fitzgerald. And in his excitement he jumped into Roaring Brook, swam over to us, and accompanied the boat back, blowing bubbles and kicking his feet.

Tired and wet, but pleased with ourselves, we sat on the bank and ate our picnic lunch.

After wolfing down a few sandwiches, Olive picked up the small boat and studied it.

She turned it over and then set it down on the moss. "I could do it," she said. "There are some standing dead oaks that would do fine, both for the framework of the boat and for the mast."

Bill nodded encouragement.

She frowned, still looking at *Heloise*. "It would have to be very big to accommodate a bear," she said.

Fitzgerald snorted. "And what are you supposed do with it once it's built?" he asked. "It will hardly fit on Roaring Brook. I suppose you could paddle it around in circles on Turtle Pond."

Cluid said, "I thought we were going to travel in it. Off the Mound."

"Right," said Fitzgerald. "And how do you propose we get it off the Mound in the first place? Carry it out the Secret Way, through the labyrinth? It wouldn't fit through the door, let alone down those tunnels. Or does it fly, too?"

"You're right," said Olive. "I hadn't thought of that."

But Bill had.

Reaching into his sack, he found a small screwdriver and a wrench. Then he went over to *Heloise*, and started dismantling the frame and pulling off the fabric covering.

"Hey!" I cried.

"No, it's all right," Olive said, watching Bill carefully. "Look, it's made to come apart! All of the pieces can be reassembled! Oh, that is clever, Bill. If we make the big boat the same way, we can take it apart to carry it through the labyrinth, and then reassemble it when we get to the river! You must have planned it that way all along!"

That was when we realized how perfect Bill's design really was.

"Looks like he's thought of everything," Fitzgerald admitted.

There was more talk about building the big boat, but I wasn't paying too much attention. I was busy having an idea of my own.

It concerned a ferry service for small animals, and picnic excursions to Frog Island. And a small house built just for me, under the ferns, with a dock where I could tie up my boat. I would become the Boatman of the Mound!

I decided to learn all I could about boats and boating.

Besides the paddles, *Heloise* had a mast and a sail. I would learn how to

use them. I would learn about currents and weather conditions, about anchors and lines and cleats. I would get myself a cap and a slicker! And I would start by looking through the books that the humans had left behind in the Cliff House library.

Pubba, Olive's father, found me there later, and he showed me a special book.

"I heard about your boat," he boomed. "And I thought you might find this useful."

It was called *Small Boat Craft*—just what I wanted!

I began reading it right away. How lucky that I had been going to the Fog Mound School and improving my reading!

Meanwhile, Olive began work on the big boat. And boating fever took over the Mound.

Fitzgerald was our reading teacher at school. He picked out a book for the class to read out loud, called *Paddle-to-the-Sea*. It was written by a human named Holling Clancy Holling. I was the first one to read:

"The Canadian wilderness was white with snow. From Lake Superior northward the evergreen trees wore hoods and coats of white. A heavy blanket of cloud hung low across the hills. There was no sound . . ."

I thought, *Oh boy, this sounds like my kind of story!* And I was right. When *Paddle* almost got sawed in half, I felt my fur stand on end. Now, that's what I call a good story! I memorized it, and later on I told it to Brown and Cluid.

It took us six days to read *Paddle-to-the-Sea*. After we finished, Fitzgerald

said he was going to read us a poem called "Sea-fever", by John Masefield.
He opened a book and began:

"I must go down to the seas again, to the lonely sea and the sky,

And all I ask is a tall ship and a star to steer her by . . ."

I don't know which I liked better—the story or the poem! Later, I wrote a
poem of my own:

On Roaring Brook

My boat lies waiting,
Where the water laps the shore.
I will go to her,
We'll sail away.
She won't be waiting anymore!

Needless to say, it was a big hit with the other students.

5

Setting Sail

53

55

BEFORE YOU GUYS CAME TO THE FOG MOUND I NEVER THOUGHT I WOULD BE GOING OUT THROUGH THE SECRET WAY AND INTO THE OUTSIDE WORLD MYSELF.

BE CAREFUL AND STAY WITH US. SOME OF THE TUNNELS LEAD TO THE DEADLY FOG PITS!

58

6

The Dark Forest

How strange to be off the Mound again, in a world without boundaries! A fresh wind ruffled my fur, and I felt happy and free.

"I must go down to the seas again!" I shouted, quoting from the John Masefield poem. "To the lonely sea and the sky!"

"Thelonious! Get back in the cockpit or put on your life preserver!" Fitzgerald said sternly. "In fact, you small animals should probably be wearing your life preservers all the time."

Brown glared at me as I hurried back into the cockpit.

"We'll be all right," I mumbled.

It was a calm day. *Big Heloise* glided smoothly down the river. The life preservers weren't mentioned again.

Cluid got out her drawing book and sketched the mountain scenery. I looked over her shoulder.

"Hey," I said. "I didn't know you were so good at drawing!"

"Do you like it?" she asked shyly.

"This is the life!" said Brown, basking in a sunny spot. "Is there anything to eat?"

All day we ate and sailed, and sunned and talked, riding the flow of the river current with the wind at our backs. Nobody had to lift a paddle. Olive manned the rudder and kept us on an even course. I told some of the legends I had learned in the Untamed Forest—*The Story of Bob*, *The Princess and the Peabrain*, and *The Wild Boar of Madagascar*.

"There are wild animals in the Untamed Forest, aren't there?" Cluid asked when I had finished The Wild Boar.

"Sure," I said. "There are lots more wild animals than talking animals. In fact, I was surprised when I discovered how many talking animals there were in the rest of the world. In the Untamed Forest *most* of the animals are wild. You can still communicate with them, you know," I explained. "You just have to use the low language."

"The low language is largely forgotten on the Fog Mound," Olive added. "But I think it would be pretty easy to pick it up."

"That's right," I said. "It's very simple—angry growls and gentle purrs. You get the idea."

"There's a lot of body language involved too," said Brown. "Watch out for wild predators who have their ears flattened and their eyes fixed on you."

"I think I'll be watching out for *all* wild predators!" Cluid cried. "Whatever their body language says."

The riverbanks were more wooded now. We were entering the Untamed Forest.

"Can you steer us over along the east bank?" I asked Olive. "There should be a small island there, and then we'll see the entrance to Serena's Cove. That's right near where I used to live, and we could put up for the night in the Rock Cave."

We followed the shoreline. Fitzgerald lay on the deck and looked down into the shallow water so he could warn Olive of any submerged obstacles. Brown and Cluid looked deep into the woods, watching for wild animals. I stared straight ahead.

"There it is!" I exclaimed. "There's Black Rice Island."

Olive folded the sail and pulled hard on the tiller, and we swung out of the flowing river and into the quiet waters of Serena's Cove.

The tree branches touched one another over our heads. It was late in the day now, almost dark. The *peep-peep* of a lone tree frog was the only sound.

"There's a small pond around the bend," I whispered to Olive, "where we can tie up the boat."

"Why are you whispering?" Cluid whispered.

"Because it's getting dark," I whispered back, "and we're in the Untamed Forest. Prey animals like us have to be very careful in the dark."

Olive paddled quietly up the narrowing stream.

We rounded a bend and startled a wild deer. She looked at us with big eyes, then bounded off into the forest.

At the far end of the pond a beaver splashed into the water.

Cluid grabbed my arm and held on, quivering.

"What was that?" she whispered.

"Just a beaver," I replied. "Don't worry."

Olive lifted her paddle out of the water and set it down inside the boat. Then she stood up carefully, keeping her feet far apart for balance, and caught hold of an overhanging branch.

The boat slowed to a stop. Olive pulled along the branch until we touched the shore.

Just then a horrible scream ripped through the forest.

Cluid gasped. Brown shrieked and launched himself across the bow, throwing his arms around my neck.

"Hey," I said quietly, pushing him off. "It's okay. That's the lynx, but she's far away. *You* ought to be used to predators, Brown. There are plenty of them in the City of Ruins. More than here, even."

Brown adjusted his shirt. "Well, yeah," he whispered, "sure there are. But I know my way around the City of Ruins. And there are lots of places to hide there—in the walls and in the rubble. Here, there's nowhere to hide!"

"Nowhere to hide? " I yelped, forgetting to keep quiet.

Then I realized we didn't have to whisper, not as long as Olive and Fitz were right there, so I went back to my normal voice.

"There are *tons* of places to hide," I said. "There are trees, stumps, stone walls, tunnels, you name it! Just watch and listen, and stay close to me."

"Oh, Thelonious," Cluid wailed. "I'm frightened!"

"Nobody's going to bother us as long as we're with Fitzgerald and Olive," I said. "Everybody should stay together, that's all."

Olive stepped out onto the shore.

"What about the boat?" she asked. "Can we leave her here, unguarded?"

"Oh, sure," I said. "There might be some curiosity, but nobody will take her. We should probably lock up the food, though."

"Speaking of food, let's take some snacks," Fitzgerald said, stuffing some food into his pack. "We might get hungry overnight."

I was excited. I jumped around a little.

I said, "You'll like the Rock Cave. It's where we get together to tell stories and stuff. And tomorrow I want you guys to meet my sister and my mom. Wait'll Dolores sees Bill. Oh boy, is she gonna flip!"

"Where *is* Bill?" asked Cluid.

I looked around. "Hey, Bill!" I called.

"Maybe he's sleeping in the boat," Brown said.

Olive lit a lamp. We turned everything out of the boat and put it back again. No Bill.

We walked back and forth along the shore, calling, "Bill! Bill!"

Cluid said, "He can't have gone far in this short time. Why doesn't he answer us?"

"Maybe he's teasing," Brown said. "Remember when we were trying to follow him and he jumped out and scared us?"

"C'mon out, Bill," I said loudly. "This isn't funny. We're in the Untamed Forest now!"

Olive held her lamp high, and we waited, all quiet and listening.

Arf! Arf! Arf! we heard in the distance.

"Foxes," I said.

We listened.

The barking stopped. The tree frog resumed its cry.

"You guys go on to your cave," Olive finally said. "I'll stay here. I'm sure Bill will turn up."

I didn't say anything, but I was pretty sure Bill wasn't going to turn up. Didn't I know, better than any of the others, how quietly and quickly a predator in the dark forest can snatch?

I led the way, feeling very low.

I should have been watching out for Bill. I should have known he was the most helpless of us all, with his white coat and his bare skin. The only human we would ever know in this life!

I almost wished it had been me instead.

"Thelonious!" Fitz called. "Is there another way? I can't fit through there."

"Oh, sorry, I wasn't thinking!"

I retraced my steps. Of *course* Fitzgerald couldn't fit through a chipmunk tunnel!

"Don't worry about Bill," Cluid whispered to me.

(How did she know I was worrying?)

"He'll be all right," she added.

I had to lead them through the open field. It's an exposed place, and I would never have ventured there in the moonlight without Fitzgerald's protection.

A silent shadow crossed the moon.

My muscles tensed.

Instinct told me to run for shelter, but reason kept me close to Fitz.

Hoo hoo! came the owl's cry.

And then a short poem came to me—a short, non-rhyming poem, like the ones Fitzgerald called "haiku." It just popped right into my head.

A warm night,

The wicked owl

Obstructs the moon.

The owl, the lynx, the foxes . . . something had gotten Bill. I shivered and tried not to think about it.

"Shhh." Cluid put her hand on my arm and stopped me. "What's that?" she whispered.

We stood stock-still, listening. Someone passed silently through the brush.

We waited.

A branch moved slightly against the moonlit sky.

A faint voice in the distance called, "Wait up!"

Closer to us, came the reply, "Well, hurry up. We'll be late for the Meet!"

I gasped. *The Meet!*

I turned to the others. "It's the full moon!" I said, gesturing to the sky. "That means it's the night of the All-Forest Meet. All the talking animals are getting together at the Rock Cave! C'mon! Now you'll get to meet everybody."

The All-Forest Meet! How could I have forgotten? That just shows you how long I had been away. There I was making up poems about the moon and making plans to sleep in the Rock Cave and everything, and I forgot that the full moon meant it was the night of the Meet!

I thought, *Oh boy! Now I can show all my new friends to all my old friends! And do I have some great tales to tell!*

7

Morrie

75

77

Return to the Ruins

"*Is that the City of Ruins?*" Cluid asked me.

I nodded, and together we stared at the distant skyline.

"What's it like there, Thelonious?" she asked.

"Well," I said, wondering how to begin. "There are buildings all along the streets, one right next to the other. A lot of them were once taller than the tallest trees in the Untamed Forest, but now most of them are falling down, so the streets are full of rubble. And everywhere you go the ground is as hard as stone. Nothing grows there, you know—nothing at all."

Cluid stared at me. "But I thought it was beautiful—full of culture, and more like . . . well, like the Fog Mound!"

"It's not agricultural like the Fog Mound," I said. "But there are amazing human artifacts just lying around for the taking. Once you get to know it," I added wisely, "you can appreciate it for the lost culture it represents."

Big Heloise swept swiftly downriver. Olive took down the sail and let the current carry us. Morrie, who had been flying overhead, landed on the mast and rode in with us.

Cluid got out her pad and pencil and started to draw. The jagged line of crumbling roofs took shape on her paper.

I wished I could draw like that.

After watching her for a while, I went and leaned against the gunwale beside Brown.

"You don't like it here, do you, Brown?" I asked him.

He looked up at the dark skyline. "I have mixed feelings," he said.

I waited, but he didn't explain.

"Do you have family here?" I finally asked him.

"No. I'm an orphan. I don't remember my mother."

"Gee, Brown—," I started.

"It's all right," he interrupted.

After a pause he added, "I was the only small lizard in the Dragon Lady's mansion. They called me Brownie." He looked disgusted.

"At first, when I was young, they treated me like a special pet, giving me yummies and saying wasn't I cute, and stuff like that.

"Then the Dragon Lady brought in a parrot named Kai to teach me reading and writing. The Dragon Lady can't read herself, you know, even though she is a talker.

"After I had learned to read and write, I convinced her that I would be most useful to her as a spy. That gave me some freedom, you see, to move around the city on my own. And she gave me a red scarf to wear— to show that I was under the protection of her ratmink army. Of course, the ratminks weren't too fond of me, but they didn't dare do anything to hurt me."

"Gee," I said again.

"Hey, don't feel sorry for me, Thelonious," Brown said. "I was a lot better off than Kai Parrot. At least I could travel around the city. I had my red scarf. I felt pretty smart. I knew everybody's secrets. I had a hideout that the ratminks didn't know about. And I had my collection of gems. Like I said, I have mixed feelings."

Brown shrugged. "Even though I had come to despise the Dragon Lady," he continued, "I hadn't thought about leaving the city—not until I overheard you guys talking about the Fog Mound. Then I made a sudden decision to break away."

I frowned at him.

"So you went away and left Kai Parrot at the mercy of the Dragon Lady?"

"Of course not," said Brown. "I let him go, just before I took off."

"Hooray!" I shouted, and I slapped Brown on the back. "You're a hero, Brown!

He said "Yeah, well, whatever . . ."

We drifted down the river until Fitzgerald said, "I think we should put in by the warehouses, Olive. Down by the old docks. Do you agree?"

"Whatever you say, Fitz." Olive picked up her paddle and guided us closer to shore.

There was a ghostly, silent atmosphere to the city. Of course, it's often foggy there, where the river meets the sea.

From the mast Morrie said, "I sense an aura of evil about this place."

"It's much more dangerous here than it is in the Untamed Forest," I whis-

pered to Cluid.

"No, it's not," said Brown.

Fitzgerald was scanning the shoreline with narrowed eyes and twitching nostrils.

Out of the corner of his mouth he said, "Slow down, Olive. I smell ratminks!"

Olive immediately dug the paddle into the water and slowed *Big Heloise* almost to a standstill.

I sniffed the air. All I could smell was the rot of the saltwater shallows.

"There!" Brown hissed. "Between the rocks!"

I didn't see anything.

Olive began back-paddling.

"*CAW!*" cried Morrie suddenly, swooping down. "Look out!"

Two ratminks jumped out from between the rocks. One arm swung through the air. There was a whining noise; a dark object flew overhead, and then, *BLAM!* The water behind us exploded!

We all hunkered down in the boat.

"What happened? What is it?" I cried.

Olive was paddling furiously back out into the middle of the wide river. More explosions followed us. *BLAM! BLAM!*

"It looks like the ratminks have discovered explosives!" Olive called out.

"And firearms!" Fitzgerald cried, pointing to a distant figure. "Get down!"

BANG, BANG!

Luckily, their aim wasn't very good. And soon we were out of range.

The two ratminks had disappeared from the shore, but we could still hear distant bangs and see the flares of occasional explosions within the city.

"Whew!" said Olive. "It looks like conditions have gotten a lot worse since we were here last."

Fitzgerald answered with a low growl. "You can thank the humans for that! You see what happens when you breed mutant animals to fight? If they haven't got any battles to keep them busy, they take up mindless violence!"

"I don't think they were bred to fight," Brown corrected him. "The humans wanted to mass-produce mink coats. Didn't you see that true mink that came down from the north a couple of years ago?"

Fitzgerald shivered. "He didn't last long," he said.

"Yeah," said Brown, "but he did have a nice coat."

"Well, I guess that was one human experiment that went wrong," I said.

"Nobody in their right mind would want a coat made out of *ratmink* fur. Yuck!"

Pointing at the foggy banks to our right, Fitzgerald told Olive to make for the inlets. "Maybe I can get ashore there and find some of my old pals," he said.

"I don't know if that's such a good idea, Fitz," Olive said. "Porcupine quills aren't much use against bullets, you know."

"That's what I'm worried about," Fitzgerald said.

"Hey!" I cried. "You don't think the ratminks could have hurt your friend Wally, do you, Fitzgerald?"

"I hope not," he answered gruffly.

Olive reluctantly agreed to go ashore, and paddled around to approach the city from the south. All eyes were on the lookout for ratmink activity, but the increasing darkness and a sticky fog that rose from the water were making it hard to see anything.

I didn't like it.

I said, "Are you sure this is safe?"

Fitz said, "The fog around here isn't deadly like it is around the Fog Mound, if that's what you mean."

Bill chuckled. "Laughing gas," he said.

We all stared at him.

"Is that what makes the fog deadly?" Cluid asked him. "Laughing gas?"

"What's laughing gas?" I asked.

Bill just smiled and looked mysterious.

The boat bumped into something solid. Bill's smile vanished as his feet slipped out from under him, sending him to the floor of the boat.

I grabbed for support. "What was that?" I cried.

"I think we just hit bottom," Olive said. "I must have missed the channel."

She pushed off with her paddle. We shot backward and then bumped again. Olive stopped paddling and peered into the mist.

"I don't know, Fitz," she said. "I can hardly tell where the shore is any-more. How familiar are you with this area?"

"Ahem," said Fitz. "Well . . . it's really Wally's territory."

"I'm afraid we're stuck," Olive said. "This place is nothing but a maze of shallow inlets in a sea of mud!"

"Tide's out," said Brown.

All eyes turned to Brown.

"What does that mean?" I said.

"The tide!" exclaimed Olive. "I forgot these were tidal waters! He means it's low tide, Thelonious, and when the tide comes in we should be able to get to shore! If the fog lets up."

"The fog comes in most evenings," Brown continued. "But it should clear out again tomorrow."

"If we're stranded in the mud," I said slowly, thinking as I spoke, "doesn't that mean the ratminks can get to us?"

"If we can't see them, they can't see us," Brown answered. "Besides, nobody in his right mind would try to walk through these mud flats."

He looked meaningfully at Fitzgerald.

Fitzgerald sighed and nodded. "Okay," he said. "I guess we wait it out."

Not having anything better to do, we all curled up and went to sleep.

9

Skullsy

OVERNIGHT THE TIDE HAS COME IN. SUNRISE FINDS THE **HELOISE** ONCE AGAIN AFLOAT.

THELONIOUS IS THE FIRST TO WAKE UP.

SNIFF SNIFF

WHEW! THIS WATER SMELLS **GROSS!**

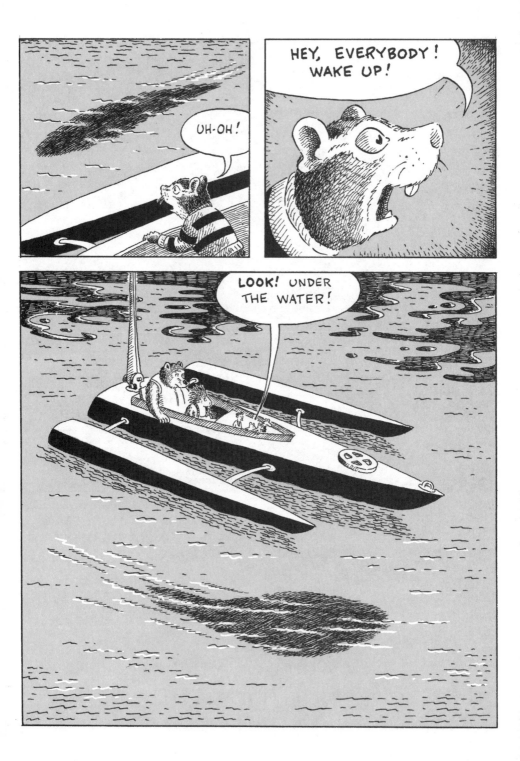

108

10

All at Sea

We left the landfill beavers and Wally behind, and we sailed away—out into the open sea—to look for Ruby and for Faradawn.

Soon there was nothing to be seen in any direction but the flat line where the water met the sky.

Big Heloise was making a small wake as she skimmed along, and all was bright and peaceful.

The boat carried us farther and farther to the east.

I spread out and let the sun soak in. *This is the life for me!* I thought.

"When do you think we'll get there?" I said to nobody in particular.

"Get where?" asked Brown.

"Well," I answered, "wherever it is that we're going."

"It would help if we knew where that was," said Fitzgerald, glaring at Bill.

Bill smiled back at him and opened his mouth to speak.

"I know," said Fitz. "East, right?"

Bill nodded happily.

"Do you think Bill really knows where we're going?" I whispered to Cluid.

"I think so. He seems to know everything," Cluid said.

"What if he's taking us somewhere we don't want to go?" whispered Brown.

His eyes bulged. "Maybe there's an island of living human scientists, still experimenting on animals. Maybe we've been handpicked for some horrible experiment!"

"Shhh," I said. "You're starting to sound like Fitzgerald."

Fitzgerald stuck his head in his basket of food.

"Anybody hungry?" he asked.

Of course we were.

We sailed on and on, and on and on. The ocean seemed endless.

"The ocean isn't endless," Olive explained. "It's got land on the other side."

"How do you know that?" Brown asked.

"From maps in human books," she answered. "Right, Fitz?"

"Well, unless things have changed since those maps were made," he replied. "We don't have any maps of the earth from after the Human Occupation, do we? Maybe that other land fell into the ocean."

"Land doesn't do that," said Olive.

"How do we know?" I piped up. "What about the lost island of Atlantis? Didn't that fall in the ocean? Or is that just a legend?"

Nobody seemed to know the answer to that one—not even Fitzgerald.

Meanwhile, our shadows were growing very long.

Olive squinted at the distant horizon. "I was hoping we would arrive someplace before dark," she said.

Morrie flew down from his perch on the mast. "No land in sight," he croaked.

"What are we going to do when it gets dark?" asked Cluid in a small voice.

"Why don't we ask Bill," Fitz suggested. "He's the one with all the solutions."

I looked around. Bill was nowhere to be seen.

"Oh no!" I cried. "Man overboard! We lost him again!"

"No, no, he's still here," said Fitzgerald. "He's rummaging around in those packages that he stowed in the hold. I'll check it out."

Fitzgerald stood up carefully and ambled to the front of the boat.

"What's up?" I heard him say to Bill.

I didn't hear any answer from Bill, but then Fitzgerald called, "Hey, look at this! He's got some charts! What are they, Bill?"

Olive stayed at the tiller, but the rest of us rushed up to see what Bill had brought. They were maps of the night sky.

Bill cleared his throat, getting ready to speak. "Olive sleep," he ordered. "All sleep."

"You." He pointed at Fitzgerald. "Bring these." He pointed at the papers.

"We sail by . . ." He pointed upward. "Stars."

Nobody had any better ideas, so we all did as Bill suggested.

It was a peaceful night, and the boat rocked us gently to sleep.

The next day dawned gray and misty.

Olive took the tiller again so Bill and Fitzgerald could rest.

We held course by the glow of the rising sun. But by midday we could no longer tell which way was which.

Bill awoke and consulted his instruments.

"Go this way, please," he said, pointing.

Olive brought the boat around.

We spent the second day making a big dent in Fitzgerald's supply of groceries.

A large fish appeared and swam close to our boat for a while. It looked at me with cold, intelligent eyes and opened its wide mouth, showing me several rows of pointed teeth.

I moved away from the side and sat in the bottom of the boat where it couldn't see me.

We were really speeding along now. I noticed that the wind had come up, and I was glad because that meant we would get wherever we were going sooner.

The motion of the boat was getting rougher. Instead of skimming along through rippling waves, we now shot up toward the sky and then came down with a smack. Then up, then *smack!* Then up, then *smack!* It was very jarring, and besides, I wasn't feeling too good. I kept remembering that last pickled beet I had eaten.

Seawater splashed over the side. Loose cans rolled from one side to the other.

And then, against the dark sky there flashed a jagged bolt of lightning, and we heard the boom of thunder that followed!

11

Byoop Bip Eekek

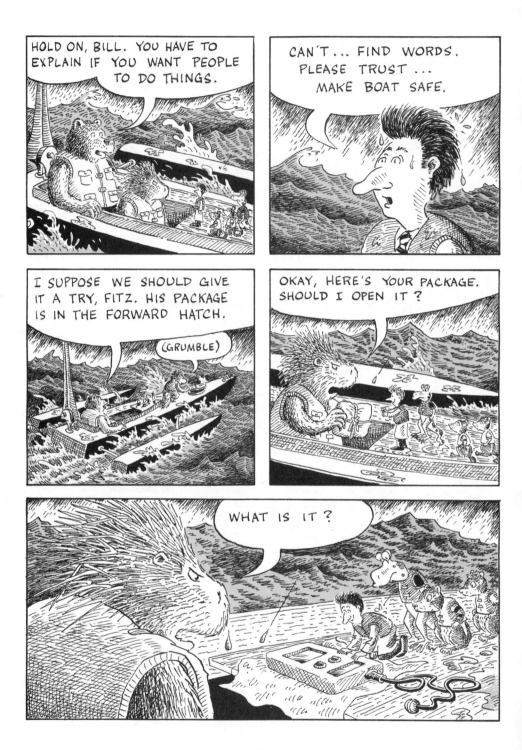

124

SEVERAL HOURS LATER—

WELL, THANKS TO BILL'S DOLPHINS, IT LOOKS LIKE WE MADE IT THROUGH THE STORM.

BOOBEEP BOOBEEP BYOOP BIP EEKEK*

*TRANSLATION: THANKS, GUYS, WE OWE YOU A LOT.

I WISH THEY DIDN'T HAVE TO GO.

12

Land Ho!

Olive unfurled the sail, and once again we were skimming over the waves. The sea still stretched to the sky in every direction. It seemed to go on forever.

I wasn't so sure I wanted to be a sailor anymore.

Brown slithered up and lay in a sunny spot beside me. The lids over his eyes almost closed.

"The food's all gone," he said.

Suddenly I felt very hungry.

"No worry," said Bill.

He tugged on another of his packages. It was marked FDF.

"Freeze-dried food," he said, pointing at the letters and looking proud of himself. "Food, for . . . months!"

Food?

I gnawed a little hole in the bag, and some powder leaked out. I sniffed it. It smelled like sawdust.

"Eat," said Bill.

I put some of the powder in my mouth. It *tasted* like sawdust too. I made a face.

Bill looked disappointed.

I ate some more, just to make him feel better.

"Well, I guess we won't starve, anyway," I said.

Bill looked happy again.

Brown was studying Bill from under his semi-closed lids. Finally he said

carefully, "We heard what you said when . . . well, before . . . that it was hard for you to find words."

Bill nodded.

He pointed to his head and said, "All . . ."

He wiggled his finger around and frowned. "Wibbly wobbly!"

"But," Brown continued, "you make some amazing things. Like this boat and that machine to call the dolphins. Your head isn't wibbly wobbly then."

Bill shook his head. Now he pointed down his throat. "Just . . . words . . . won't come out."

"You're getting much better at it, Bill," I said. "All you need is some practice."

Fitzgerald was listening to us.

"How did you know how to talk to the dolphins, Bill?" he said.

"Ah!" said Bill. "My . . . sp— . . . sp— . . ." He looked around. "You say," he said to me.

"But I don't know what you mean," I said. "Your what?"

Bill thought for a while. Then he said, "What I do. Own job."

"Specialty?" said Olive from the back of the boat.

"Yes!" Bill jumped up, pointed at Olive, and put his finger on his nose. "Ha, ha!" He pointed from Olive to his nose. "Specialty!" he repeated. "Specialty!"

"Why is he pointing at his nose?" I asked nobody in particular.

"It's charades!" piped up Cluid. "It's a game we play. You act things out without speaking, and when somebody guesses the right word, you put your finger on your nose! Bill must have played charades too."

She had a thought. "Hey! I wonder if he taught it to the animals, you know, way back, before . . . well, when he built the Fog Mound. That is, if he . . ." Her voice kind of faded away.

Fitzgerald wasn't interested in games just now. "Your specialty is talking to dolphins?" he asked Bill.

Bill sat down again. He shook his head. "Animals," he corrected Fitz. "All animals."

"I see," said Fitz.

Bill beamed. "Talk to animals!" He pointed to all of us. "And animals talk to me!

"Talk like humans!" he added.

Fitzgerald leaned forward. "You mean," he said, "you got animals to talk like humans? How did you do that?"

Bill said, "And thumbs! Give animals thumbs!" He pointed at Fitzgerald's thumb.

Uh-oh.

Fitzgerald drew back away from Bill and swelled up so that his quills stuck out through his fur.

"So what are you telling us?" he said in an awful voice. "You were a sci-entist who made genetic changes in animals so they would have thumbs and talk like humans?"

"LAND HO!" cried Morrie from the top of the mast. "LAND HO!"

13

The Island

135

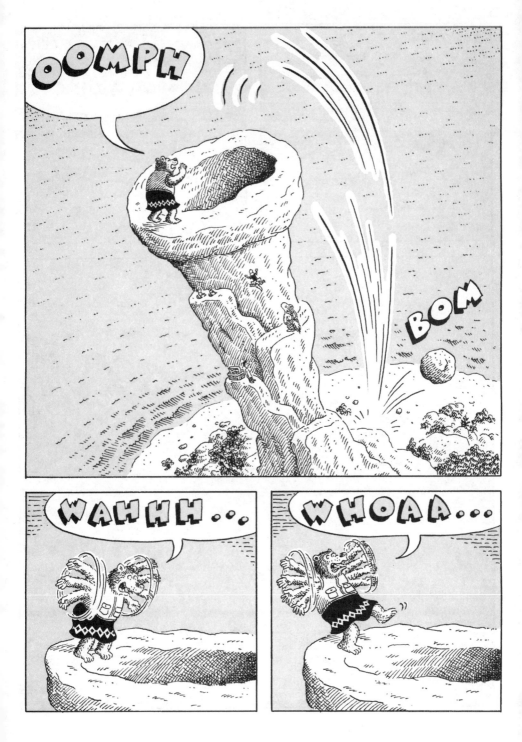

141

14

The Birds of
Faradawn Island

Cluid, Brown, and I

slid as fast as we could back down the mountain. To us, big birds meant one thing— *danger!*

The birds kept on coming, spewing out like lava and then drifting down to settle in the trees, on the rocks, on the sand . . .

There was no place to hide!

We rolled and slid, hoping speed would make us hard to catch. When we hit flat ground, I pulled Cluid under a big leaf and we lay there trembling.

The big birds landed all around us.

Brown wasn't so lucky. When I peeked out, I could see him flattened against the rocky base of the volcano, trying to blend in. I didn't think much of his chances.

The wind of settling wings ruffled our leaf, but I held it down by the edges.

Then a big hooked claw landed on the dirt beside us. I held my breath.

147

Our leaf was torn from my grasp and tossed aside.

And there we were, more exposed than Brown, even!

Trembling, we faced a group of staring big-beaked birds.

"Have no fear," one bird said to us. "We are gentle birds. We want to thank you, not harm you."

"WE WANT TO THANK YOU!" all the birds chorused.

Many of the birds were brightly colored, but not all. Some were small and brown—more like the common birds in the Untamed Forest.

Brown inched his way down the volcano and scuttled over to join us.

"They just want to thank us," I whispered to him.

"I heard," he said. "That's why I came down. Besides," he added, "this one is a parrot. Like my friend Kai, remember?"

Brown squawked a few words in what I assumed was parrot talk, and the parrot bobbed up and down and squawked back.

Morrie landed beside us, holding Bill by the trousers. Olive and Fitzgerald were making their own way slowly down the mountain.

More birds crowded around, all chattering and cooing.

"Thank you. THANK YOU!"

"Welcome. Welcome to Faradawn Island."

"We would have starved. STARVED! STARVED!"

". . . the giant Rock-Pusher . . ."

". . . the Whopper . . ."

". . . the evil crab mutants . . ."

"THANK YOU! THANK YOU! THANK YOU!"

And more and more, all around us, until I felt like they might as well have eaten us, because we were about to be thanked to death anyway. But gradually all their voices faded out, and the birds near us cocked their heads to listen to something else—loud, distressed calls coming from the rocks beyond the mountain.

"What's going on over there?" I asked Morrie. "I can't understand what they're saying."

"That's because it's bird talk," Morrie said. "They're saying . . . hold on . . . it sounds like, 'Crabs in the orchard!' Does that make sense?"

The call was taken up by the birds around us, some in bird talk and some in our language. "Crabs in the orchard! *SQUAWK! CAW! WAK!* Crabs in the orchard! *SKREEE! SKREEE!*" All at once they took to the air and flew off in the direction of the original cries.

Naturally we ran after them to see what was happening.

What we found was a sheltered orchard of old, gnarled fruit trees heavy with ripe fruit. Crabs were swarming all over the orchard, even up in the trees, crunching and sucking down all the luscious fruits.

Some of the birds were using their beaks and talons to pick up the crabs, one by one, and drop them back into the ocean. But the crabs kept trying to pinch the birds' feet with their nasty claws.

Olive quickly stepped out of her skirt and used it to scoop up a number of crabs. She carried them to a rock that overhung the water and dumped them out.

"Let me help you," Fitzgerald called. He grasped one of the sharp quills from his tail and began herding a crab toward Olive, jabbing at its undersides with the quill.

I picked up a small rock and hurled it at a crab that was climbing up one of the fruit trees.

It turned a cold look in my direction and continued to climb. I could see

by its eyes that it wasn't an ordinary wild crab but some kind of horrible, intelligent mutant.

Several more of them turned to look at me.

I took a few steps back.

One of them said something in a

language I couldn't understand, and all the crabs that were close to me started moving sideways in my direction.

I turned and ran. Cluid and Brown saw me coming and didn't wait to see what it was all about. We scrambled, hearts pounding, back the way we had come, until at last I sensed there was no one following anymore. A quick look back assured me that the crabs had returned to the orchard.

"It's okay!" I called to the others. "They've stopped chasing."

We scrambled up a boulder and watched from above, unable to help. There are times when you just have to accept that size matters.

A very small blue and yellow bird settled near us. "The crab mutants are stealing our fruit," she said. Her voice was very loud and clear. She sounded angry.

"My name is Jenny," she added. "And it's *our* fruit! We cultivate the trees. We plant them and water them. We prune them with our beaks and fertilize them with our droppings."

"That sounds like the Fog Mound!" Cluid exclaimed. "We grow our own food too!"

Jenny bobbed her head up and down and continued, "Some of us eat the fruit, and some of us eat the seeds, and the leaves feed our herds of caterpillars and moths, which we also eat. It's a very good system, and it's not right for the crabs to steal our fruit when they don't do any of the work!"

"These crabs," I said. "Did you say they were mutants?"

"Yes!" Jenny bobbed. "Aren't they awful? They're intelligent and evil! They tried to kill us, you know, by trapping us in Mount Yo!"

"You don't mean they put that huge rock up there!" I couldn't believe that!

She sighed. "It used to be so peaceful here. Our orchards produced fruit and caterpillars and moths for us to eat, and we've been able to sustain it for years and years—just the way Mary the Founder had taught our ancestors."

"Who's Mary the Founder?" I asked.

"Mary the Founder was a human. She brought our ancestors here and taught them everything they would need to know in order to survive after the Human Occupation."

"We think the Fog Mound was made for the same reason," Cluid said shyly. "Did Mary make genetic changes in the birds so they could speak?"

"Why would she do that?" Jenny asked. "Birds could always speak. Mary just taught them the human language."

Brown had been watching the birds below as they battled with the odious crabs. "We're winning!" he said. "That's the last of the crabs, thrown back in the ocean. WAY TO GO, GUYS!" he yelled, pumping his fist in the air.

The rest of us looked down into the orchard. The big birds and animals seemed to be rewarding themselves by eating some of the fruit they had saved, so we climbed down to join them.

I introduced Olive and Fitzgerald to Jenny.

"Where's Bill?" I asked, looking around.

"I think he's with Morrie," Olive answered.

"Bill?" said Jenny clearly. "Did you say Bill?"

"Bill?" repeated some of the other birds. "BILL? BILL?"

"Yeah," I said. "He's with us. And Morrie, too."

"BILL? BILL? BILL?"

The name passed from bird to bird until the whole orchard resounded with it.

Luckily, Morrie flew up then, with Bill dangling from his beak.

He set his human passenger down.

"Does somebody want Bill?" he said.

A very large bird pushed his way up to us. "Is there a Bill here?" he squawked.

"This is Bill," Olive said, standing beside him in a protective way.

The big bird leaned over and peered at Bill. His eyes widened. He gave Bill a long, unblinking stare.

"This?" the bird finally said.

Bill grinned at him. The rest of us nodded. "Yes," said Olive. "His name is Bill. Why do you ask?"

Instead of answering her, the bird looked around at his fellow birds. Several of them nodded.

"We didn't think he would be so small," the big bird finally said. "I am Mitchko. I will take you to Bill Rock."

Now it was our turn to be surprised. Bill Rock?

The other birds flew up into the sky, but Mitchko turned and walked away, stopping to wait so we could catch up. We followed him.

He took us out of the orchard and along an overgrown trail to a small clearing behind the house.

"Bill Rock," he announced, using his claws to pull aside some vines that were covering an old concrete slab.

Carved into the concrete were the letters B I L L. And below that, M A T T A K E U N K I N S T I T U T E.

What did it mean?

I looked over at Bill. He climbed up on the slab and traced out the letters in his name with his finger. Then he turned to Mitchko and said, "From Mary?"

Mary? I thought. *Had Bill known this Mary the Founder? The one who taught the birds how to plant their orchard? He must have. That would explain why he wanted to come to Faradawn in the first place.*

Mitchko bobbed his head up and down. "It's a message for Bill," he said.

Bill traced the other letters and looked puzzled. Then he got down on his hands and knees and pulled at the vines and grasses that were growing over the concrete. Cluid and I climbed up to help. And Mitchko scraped at them with a large claw.

Soon we had revealed more of the message!

JOIN US

TIME IS NO OBSTACLE

I didn't feel any wiser, but Bill stood up and smiled broadly, first at Mitchko and then at the whole bird congregation. Then he lifted both arms and bowed.

In response the birds rose up as one and called out in their various bird voices.

Jenny landed near me again.

"They're happy that Bill has come and received his message from Mary the Founder," she explained. "And grateful that Olive was able to free us from the big rock. They think that fate has smiled on our island and that we should hold a Wingfest in celebration!"

"What's a Wingfest?" I said.

15

Wingfest

163

THE SEAGULLS LOVED THAT ONE.

PAY ATTENTION TO THIS NEXT ONE, OLIVE. IT'S **MITCHKO THE OSPREY!**

165

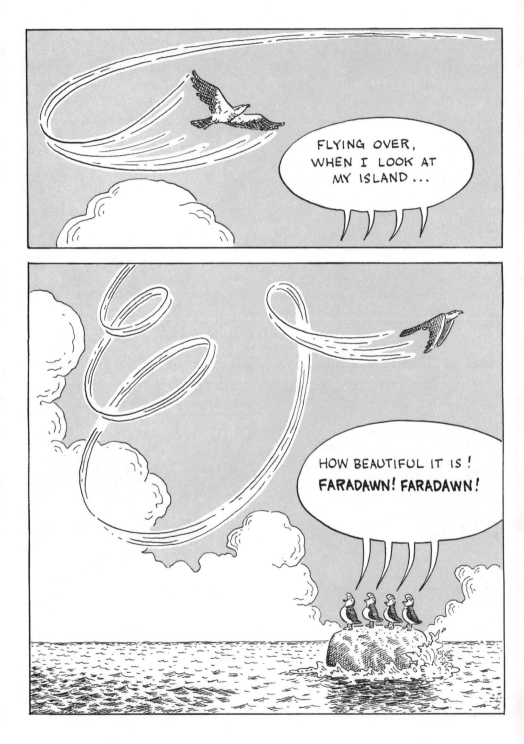

170

16

The Whopper

It was the biggest creature I had ever seen.

At the sight of it all the birds took to the air, squawking and screeching. They made a tremendous, deafening noise, but the Whopper just kept on rising up out of the sea.

"Run for your lives! Run!" Mitchko screamed at us from the air. "Flee from the evil Whopper!"

We ran.

A black claw, bigger than the whole of Olive, opened wide, then snapped down on the thick branches that made up the nestatorium, crushing them as if they were the smallest twigs. Two more snaps and the whole nestatorium crumbled to bits and fell into the deep water below.

We just barely made it out in time!

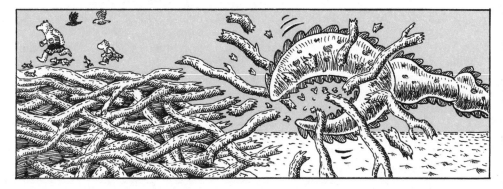

Olive leaped from ledge to boulder looking back over her shoulder. Morrie flew right behind her with Bill dangling from his beak. We Smalls did our best, scooting into the crevices for cover. And Fitz brought up the rear with his quills all standing out and his dangerous tail swishing back and forth.

The Whopper came after us, pushing big boulders out of his way with ease.

I was worried about Fitz. He wasn't very fast, and I wasn't sure his quills could save him this time.

"Go on!" he yelled in an angry voice, waving his paw at us. "I'll catch up."

Mitchko and his friends circled overhead and repeatedly dive-bombed the big monster. It distracted the monster long enough for Fitzgerald to gain a little ground, even though the birds' sharp claws just glanced uselessly off the tough crab shell.

"FLEE! FLEE!" Mitchko called to us.

The Whopper's claws waved about in the air, reaching for the birds that were swooping over him.

We fled as fast as we could.

Mitchko flew over us and called out, "We cannot stop the Whopper! We must surrender our beautiful island. You too must leave."

And then he and his friends veered out to sea.

I looked and was horrified to see that all the other birds were already far away, flying away from us, out over the ocean.

They were deserting Faradawn! And they were deserting *us*!

But all was not lost.

We still had *Big Heloise*, tied up where the water lapped the shore, waiting to take us away! I could see her mast swaying above the gentle waves.

We did not hesitate.

The giant crab was no longer behind us, but none of us believed he would give up so easily. Even now, he might be sneaking up behind the house, or around the rocks, or *anything*! No, it would be best for us to leave, and to leave as quickly as possible.

We hurried toward the boat.

Olive untied *Big Heloise*'s line and started pulling her in.

Morrie picked Bill up again and hovered above, ready to deposit him in the cockpit.

I looked around. The Whopper was nowhere in sight. The island looked strangely peaceful. I sighed. Mary the Founder had picked such a nice place for her birds.

"It's so sad that the birds have to leave their island!" I said.

"Yeah," said Brown, "but it's not so sad for *us* to have to leave it. Let's get out of here before that giant crab shows up again.

"Hey, you know something?" he added. "I'll bet it was the Whopper who put that rock on top of the mountain!"

"I guess he could do it, all right," I agreed.

"I'll be glad to get away from here," Olive said.

She was just hauling in the boat when, with a huge splash, the water parted and a giant open claw reached up out of the water!

"YOW!" I sputtered as water splashed over me. It would have washed me right off the rock if I hadn't grabbed hold of Olive's foot fur and hung on.

When I shook the salty water out of my eyes, I saw the claw lifting *Big*

Heloise right out of the water. *CRUNCK!* The claw snapped shut, crunching our beautiful boat into pieces!

"NO!" I cried.

But it was done. Our boat was gone. We were trapped on the island, and there was no escape!

Olive picked up a stick and faced the huge monster. Anyone could see it was no use. But we weren't giving in without a fight!

17

Attack of the Crocodiles

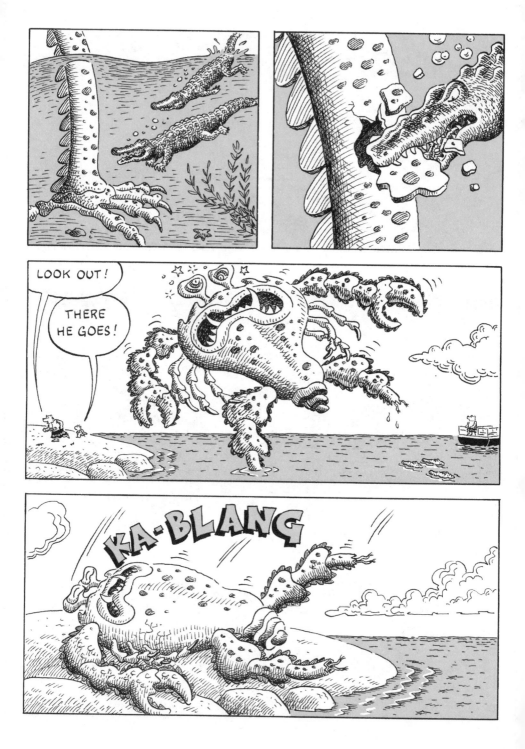

188

195

About the Author and Illustrator

Susan Schade and **Jon Buller**, a husband-and-wife team, have worked together on many previous books for children. Jon does the illustrating and Susan writes the stories. For the Fog Mound trilogy, Jon went back to what first sparked his interest in drawing—comics. They live in Lyme, Connecticut.

ALADDIN GOES GRAPHIC!

COMING SOON:

THE CHRONICLES OF
ARTHUR
SWORD OF FIRE AND ICE

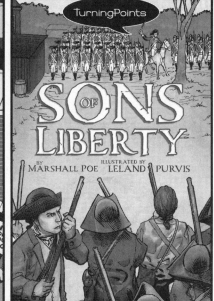
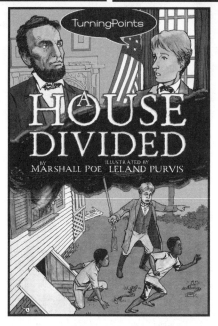